Carlos & Carmen

The Sweet Treasure

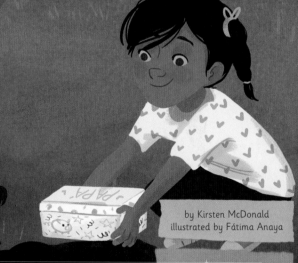

by Kirsten McDonald
illustrated by Fátima Anaya

Calico Kid
An Imprint of Magic Wagon
abdobooks.com

For Mick, Doug, Kirk, Arthur, Milton, Jeremy, Ernie, Owen,
and all the other great dads! —KKM

Para mi tierra, El Salvador. —FA

abdobooks.com

Published by Magic Wagon, a division of ABDO, PO Box 398166, Minneapolis, Minnesota 55439. Copyright © 2020 by Abdo Consulting Group, Inc. International copyrights reserved in all countries. No part of this book may be reproduced in any form without written permission from the publisher. Calico Kid™ is a trademark and logo of Magic Wagon.

Printed in the United States of America, North Mankato, Minnesota.
052019
092019

THIS BOOK CONTAINS
RECYCLED MATERIALS

Written by Kirsten McDonald
Illustrated by Fátima Anaya
Edited by Bridget O'Brien
Design Contributors: Christina Doffing & Candice Keimig

Library of Congress Control Number: 2018964980

Publisher's Cataloging-in-Publication Data

Names: McDonald, Kirsten, author. | Anaya, Fátima, illustrator.
Title: The sweet treasure / by Kirsten McDonald; illustrated by Fátima Anaya.
Description: Minneapolis, Minnesota : Magic Wagon, 2020. | Series: Carlos & Carmen
Summary: Carlos and Carmen come up with a treasure hunt to make this year's Father's Day really special for Papá.
Identifiers: ISBN 9781532134944 (lib. bdg.) | ISBN 9781532135545 (ebook) | ISBN 9781532135842 (Read-to-Me ebook)
Subjects: LCSH: Hispanic American families—Juvenile fiction. | Twins—Juvenile fiction. | Brothers and sisters—Juvenile fiction. | Father's Day—Juvenile fiction.
Classification: DDC [E]—dc23

Table of Contents

Chapter 1
The Plan

Carlos and Spooky tiptoed into Carmen's room.

"Wake up," Carlos whispered.

"Mmmuhh," Carmen mumbled.

"Come on, Carmen," Carlos said. "We've got stuff to do today."

"Huhuhh," Carmen grumbled.

Carlos said, "Mañana is Father's Day, and we have nada planned."

Spooky crept down the bed and pounced on Carmen's feet.

Carmen's eyes flew open. She sat up quickly.

"Let's make a Día del Padre plan," Carlos said.

Carmen was wide awake now. She said, "It needs to be a fun plan."

"With everything Papá likes," said Carlos.

"Like puzzles," said Carmen.

"And treasure," said Carlos.

"And ice cream," added Carmen. "Helado is Papá's favorite."

The twins thought and thought.

"We could bury some helado and treasure hunt for it," said Carmen.

"I think the helado would get all melty," said Carlos.

The twins thought some more. Off in the distance, they heard the ice cream truck's bell.

Suddenly Carlos looked at Carmen, and Carmen looked at Carlos.

"Are you thinking what I'm thinking?" they said.

And, because they were twins, they were.

Chapter 2
More Money

Carlos and Carmen got their piggy banks. They shook out their money. "We need more dinero," said Carmen.

The twins looked at each other and smiled.

"And we know just where to look," said Carlos.

"¡Vámonos!" said Carmen.

The twins ran to the living room. Carlos found coins underneath the sofa cushions. Carmen found coins under the sofa.

Next, they ran to the kitchen. Carmen found coins in the junk drawer. Carlos even found two quarters and a penny under the refrigerator.

Last, the twins went out to the car. They looked under the seats and between the seats. They looked under the car mats and in all of the cup holders.

Carmen found her mittens, and Carlos found his flashlight. And, they both found lots of coins.

The twins ran up to Carmen's room and emptied out their pockets. They looked at the pile of money.

"It's not a ton of dinero," said Carlos.

"But I think it's enough," said Carmen.

15

Chapter 3
Buried Treasure

After breakfast, the twins started
to race back upstairs.

"What's the hurry, mis hijos?"
Mamá asked.

"What are you up to?" asked Papá.

"Nada," said Carmen.

"It's a sorpresa," said Carlos.

"Hmm," said their parents. But, before Mamá or Papá could ask anything else, the twins dashed upstairs.

They gathered all of the coins
and put them in a plastic box. They
made Father's Day cards and added
those to the box. Then they ran back
downstairs with their box.

"Now what are you up to?" asked
Papá.

This time Carmen said, "It's a
sorpresa," and Carlos said, "Nada."

"But don't come outside, Papá,"
said Carmen.

"And, no peeking out the window,"
added Carlos.

The twins raced onto the deck and
grabbed their shovels. They ran to a
corner of the backyard. They dug and
dug and dug.

When the hole was big enough, they dropped in the box. They covered the box with dirt and sprinkled leaves on the dirt. Then they used sticks to mark the spot with an *X*.

"Should we make a map or write clues for Papá?" Carlos asked.

"Let's do a bunch of pistas," said Carmen.

The twins ran back inside and upstairs to Carmen's room. They wrote clues on pieces of paper. They folded up the clues and wrote numbers on them.

"Now let's hide these pistas for Papá to find," said Carmen.

"¡Vámonos!" said Carlos.

Chapter 4
Under the X

The next day Carlos and Carmen ran into their parents' room. "Happy Día del Padre," the twins said.

"We have a sorpresa for you," said Carmen.

"It's a treasure hunt," said Carlos. "With lots of pistas."

"I love treasure hunts with lots of clues," said Papá.

Carlos gave Papá the first clue. It said, "Look under a pillow."

Papá looked under his pillow, but nothing was there. He looked under Mamá's pillow, but nothing was there either. Then he looked under Carlos's pillow and found the next clue.

The twins followed Papá as he found the clues. There were clues on the stairs, under coffee cups, and in cupboards.

The last clue was taped to Spooky's collar. It said, "Dig at the X."

"Hmm," said Papá. "I can't think of an X."

"Maybe look by the fence," suggested Carlos.

"We can help you," said Carmen.

"¡Vámonos!" said Papá.

The twins grabbed Papá's hands
and led him to the *X*.

"You'll need this," said Carlos,
handing his shovel to Papá.

Papá dug and dug and dug. At last
he scooped out the plastic box.

"Open it!" said the twins.

Papá opened the box. He took out
two Father's Day cards decorated
with ice cream cones.

"Happy Día del Padre!" Carlos and Carmen shouted.

"We were going to bury some helado," said Carlos.

"But we knew it would melt," Carmen added.

"So we buried some dinero instead," said Carlos.

"And, you can get helc___ ___m the ice cream truck," j___

Papá jiggled the box. He said, "I think there's enough dinero for more than one helado. Do you know anyone else who likes ice cream?"

"Me!" shouted Carlos and Carmen.

"Then let's get some Father's Day ice cream," said Papá.

And, that's just what they did.

Spanish to English

Día del Padre – Father's Day

dinero – money

helado – ice cream

Mamá – Mommy

mañana – tomorrow

mis hijos – my children

nada – nothing

Papá – Daddy

pista – clue

sorpresa – su

¡Vámono